NOT A CAT IN SIGHT

For Penny – F.S.

For Marah – E.O'N.

SIMON & SCHUSTER

First published in Great Britain in 2022 by Simon & Schuster UK Ltd
1st Floor, 222 Gray's Inn Road, London WC1X 8HB
Text copyright © 2022 Frances Stickley • Illustrations copyright © 2022 Eamonn O'Neill
A CIP catalogue record for this book is available from the British Library upon request

ISBN: 978-1-3985-0894-1 (HB) • ISBN: 978-1-3985-0893-4 (PB) • ISBN: 978-1-3985-0895-8 (eBook)
Printed in China • 10 9 8 7 6 5 4 3 2 1

NOT A CAT IN SIGHT

FRANCES STICKLEY   **EAMONN O'NEILL**

SIMON & SCHUSTER
London   New York   Sydney   Toronto   New Delhi

No paws.
No purr.
No balls of fur.

No catnip on the floor.

A perfect day to dream, thought Mouse.
A perfect day to play.
Imagine what could happen
on a day just like today.

"Roll up for the circus!"
cried the mighty little mouse.

"And see me scale the tightrope
as I hop from house to house!"

He teetered and he toppled
and he squeaked with sheer delight . . .

as he walked along the washing line
with **not** a cat in sight.

"Or better yet, a skydiver!
And ready,
steady . . . go!"
Mouse prepared his parachute and cried,

"Geronimo!"

He leapt and laughed and marvelled
as he suddenly took flight . . .

and he landed in the compost heap
with **not** a cat in sight.

"But wait!" cried Mouse.

"What's under here?

A jewel from long ago?

A diamond or

a treasure chest?

A golden crown or . . . oh.

It's just a bone," he sighed,
and pulled it up
with all his might . . .

then raced towards the garden pond
with **not** a cat in sight.

"Perhaps I'll be a pirate!
Call me Captain Squeaky Paws!
But, avast! Beware, me hearties,
there be sharks in these 'ere shores!"

He rode a wayward whale, though it put up quite a fight . . .

as they tumbled over ocean waves
with **not** a cat in sight.

I could be a bird, thought Mouse,

and **soar** *across the sky.*

Just floating on a cloud

as all the world passes me by.

And all the Earth beneath me
seems so far away and small.

On such a lovely day,
I could be anything at all.

When the world is fine and fabulous,

the sky is blue
and bright . . .

. . . and the day is warm

and **wonderful** . . .

. . . with **not** a cat in sight.

Mouse was feeling fabulous.
The sky was blue and bright.
The day was warm and wonderful,
with **not** a cat in sight.

No whiskers in
the wardrobe.

No scratching at
the door.